I AM ARACHNE

BY ELIZABETH SPIRES

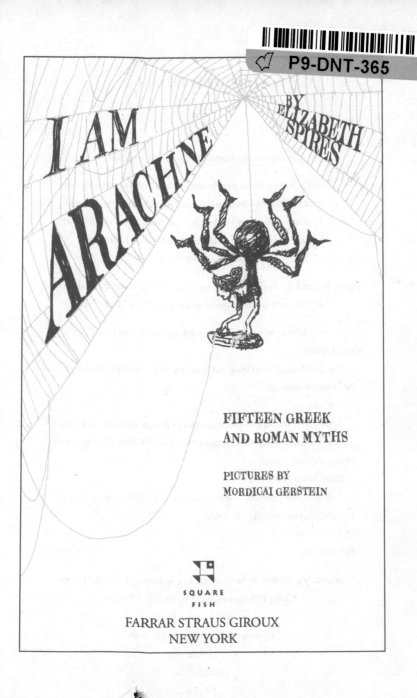

FIFTEEN GREEK
AND ROMAN MYTHS

PICTURES BY
MORDICAI GERSTEIN

SQUARE
FISH

FARRAR STRAUS GIROUX
NEW YORK

FOR JOSEPHINE AND CELIA

SQUARE
FISH

An imprint of Macmillan Publishing Group, LLC

Library of Congress Cataloging-in-Publication Data
Spires, Elizabeth.
  I am Arachne: Fifteen Greek and Roman myths / Elizabeth Spires; pictures
by Mordicai Gerstein.
    p. cm.
  Summary: A retelling of fifteen Greek and Roman myths from the point of
view of the main protagonist. Includes "Arachne," "Callisto," "Baucis and
Philemon," and "Sisyphus."
  ISBN: 978-0-312-56125-3
  1. Mythology, Classical—Juvenile literature. [1. Mythology, Classical.]
I. Gerstein, Mordicai, ill.   II. Title.
BL725 S56 2001
813'.54—dc21   00-036352

Originally published in the United States by Farrar, Straus and Giroux
Square Fish logo designed by Filomena Tuosto
Designed by Abby Kagan
First Square Fish Edition: July 2009

19   21   20   18

mackids.com

AR: 5.0

AUTHOR'S NOTE

Most of the myths in this book originated in ancient Greece and were retold, centuries later, by the Romans. In twelve of the stories included here I've used the Greek names for the gods except when a specific Roman name seemed more resonant or familiar for a contemporary reader. Three of the stories—"Pomona and Vertumnus," "Ceyx and Halcyone," and "Baucis and Philemon"—are based on lively Roman versions. In those three stories, the Roman names of the gods are used. A "Cast of Characters and Places" at the end of this book cross-references the names of the Greek gods and goddesses with their Roman counterparts.

E . S .

CONTENTS

I AM ARACHNE

ARACHNE

SPINNING, I can't stop spinning, so stay a minute, and I, Arachne, will spin a story for you . . .

Long ago, I was a simple girl who lived in the country. I wasn't beautiful or rich, but I had one great talent—I could spin and weave better than anyone in the world. Soon word got out, and travelers came from far and wide to watch me at my loom, marveling at my skill.

I admit that the attention made me a little vain. I began to boast that I was more skilled at weaving than the goddess Athena, and that was a mistake!

Soon after that, a bent old woman showed up at my doorstep, wrapped from head to toe in a tattered gray cloak. She leaned heavily on a cane and pointed a long, bony finger at my nose.

"Are you Arachne?" she asked in a raspy voice. When I said yes, she said, "I have heard that you spin better than

Athena. Can this be so? Weigh your words carefully, my girl, before you answer yes or no."

With a toss of my head, I made my boast, that yes, I could outdo Athena in any spinning contest.

Suddenly there was a terrific flash and a BANG!

The old woman's cloak lay in a crumpled heap on the ground, and there stood Athena, absolutely furious. I should have apologized that very second, but foolishly I didn't, so she challenged me to a contest.

Athena went first. With shimmering gold and silver threads, she wove a tapestry of all the gods and goddesses on Olympus, resplendent on their thrones. They seemed to breathe, they were that real, and I wondered how on earth I could do better.

Weave, weave, what could I weave? Suddenly I knew. I looked out the window and wove a tapestry of spring—red-lipped roses, tulips graceful as swans, flowering dogwoods, winding blue-green rivers, rolling meadows, and stately mountains. Why, the flowers alone looked so real that a butterfly flew in the room and tried to suck the nectar from one!

Oh, I almost forgot. I put myself in the picture as a beautiful young maiden wearing a golden crown, as if I were a goddess, too. Yes, that's what vanity will do. I'm sure my tapestry was as good as Athena's. (I won't say better, but it might have been.)

But it didn't matter. A mortal should NEVER challenge a god. If I've learned one thing, I've learned that. Athena was so angry when she saw my beautiful scene that she destroyed it with one well-aimed lightning bolt. Then she beat me over the head with her shuttle.

"Foolish, vain Arachne, will you never learn!" she screamed. "You want to spin? You'll spin all right until you die, your lines a silken trap for things that creep and fly."

And with her words, I began to shrink, until my body was no bigger than a thumb, my eyes two dots in a tiny head. Horrified, I looked down and counted eight legs instead of two, all black as night.

Spin, spin, you foolish girl, the words whirled in my brain. And dizzy, I knew that I must spin.

So now I spin my tale for *you.* See what I have spun? A web of words, a beautiful web. Do you like what I've done? My lines glisten and shimmer like diamonds in the sun.

Oh, don't worry. I've learned my lesson. Always now I bow to Athena, the greatest weaver. I am Arachne. I must spin.

PANDORA

Flies! Wasps! Mosquitoes!
Measles! Mumps! Chicken pox!
Hunger! Thirst! Cold!
Doubt! Greed! Despair!
Poverty! Plague! War!

HAVE YOU EVER WONDERED why the world is so full of suffering, big and small? Well, some say I'm to blame for everything. That's right, me, Pandora, whose name means "the gift of all." I was fashioned by the gods in heaven to be as beautiful as Aphrodite, then sent down to earth to marry Epimetheus, the brother of Prometheus. Zeus even gave me a wedding present—a beautiful box, locked, with a golden key.

But it was all a trick. You see, Zeus was angry at Prometheus for stealing fire from heaven and giving it to men on earth. So he decided to punish humankind.

Prometheus warned Epimetheus *never* to accept a gift from Zeus. But the minute Epimetheus saw me, he couldn't turn me away.

But was it fair, I ask you, for Zeus to tell me I must *never* open that mysterious box?

I remember his words exactly.

"Pandora," Zeus said. "I want you to take this box down to earth. And whatever you do, *don't look inside.*"

"Why not?" I brazenly asked.

"Impertinent girl!" scolded Zeus. "Just do what I say, and don't ask questions!"

Well, I'm no more curious than the next person. What would you have done? My first few days on earth, I resisted the temptation to open the box, though it filled my waking thoughts and dreams. Oh, occasionally, I'll admit, when my husband was sleeping, I'd take the box down from the shelf and gently shake it.

And when I did, I heard a strange hum, which only made me more curious. It sounded like a choir of mosquitoes, flat and off-key, singing to me, only to me. Finally I couldn't stand it anymore. I just *had* to see what was inside.

I took the key (I wore it on a gold chain around my neck) and slipped it into the keyhole. But the minute the key touched the lock, sparks began to fly! A puff of black smoke filled the room, and the lid snapped open with a *crack!*, as if lightning had struck.

Then, horror of horrors, a swarm of dark buzzing things

flew out—ten thousand or so—screeching and humming. They bit my arms and legs and, like a bunch of harpies, hissed terrible things in my ear:

"You stupid, evil girl!"
"Why, what possessed you?"
"Now you're in trouble!"
"Wait until Zeus hears what you did!"
"Beauty can't get you out of this one, Pandora."
"Ha! 'The gift of all.' We'll see about that."

Frightened, I began to cry. But after a few minutes, the air began to clear. The worst of them—Hunger, Plague, War, and Despair—flew out the window, to where I didn't know. (I found out later they spread to all four corners of the globe.)

And that's when I saw Hope cowering at the bottom of the box, holding its gossamer wings over its ears, trying to drown out the terrible things it had heard.

Now, Hope is a hard thing to describe, but I'll try. Hope flutters like a bird, is clear as spring water, and as constant as a star. Without Hope, our hearts would be heavy as lead. How Hope had stood being locked up in a box with that vile crowd, I'll never know.

Afraid that Hope, too, might escape, I quickly snapped the lid shut. Who knew what Doubt and Despair would do to Hope out in the world?

Sometimes now, I listen at the keyhole and hear Hope singing in the dark. Its voice is high and clear, as if an inch-high angel were singing a solo:

I am Hope,
I'm white and true.
Believe me
When I tell you,
All pain will cease,
The worst night end.
I'm Hope,
Unfailing friend!

Knowing that Hope is with me, I feel better about what happened. Everyone makes mistakes, right? I think—no, I *hope!*—that despite the suffering I've caused, everything will turn out all right in the end.

I'll never give up Hope. It's my one consolation, and it's yours, too. Anytime you want to borrow Hope, you can. Just keep it close to your heart, and don't let it fly off!

KING MIDAS

WHEN I WAS BORN, a procession of ants streamed single file up the side of my cradle, each carrying a grain of wheat. Carefully, they placed the golden grains between my lips as I slept. A seer told my parents this was an omen of the great wealth that would come to me when I was king.

The prophecy came true. I grew up to rule Phrygia, a land of fragrant roses. My gardens were famous everywhere. One night a drunk old satyr named Silenus, a friend and schoolteacher to Bacchus, the god of wine, wandered off from a party Bacchus was giving deep in the forest. Silenus fell asleep under one of my rosebushes, and I found him there the next morning, too sick to go home. For a week Silenus stayed with me, drinking my best wine and telling wonderful stories, before I took him back to Bacchus.

Bacchus was grateful for the hospitality I'd shown his friend. He said, "Midas, it was good of you to entertain

Silenus so royally. You deserve a reward. What would you like?"

Only one thing came to mind.

"*Gold!*" I blurted out. "I'd like everything I touch to turn to gold."

"You're sure about this?" asked Bacchus, startled. "Wouldn't you rather have health or happiness? Or wisdom, perhaps? I've noticed that wisdom, among mortals, is always in short supply."

I shook my head. "No, gold is the thing for me." Quickly I added, "Twenty-four-carat, of course."

"Mortals," sighed Bacchus under his breath. "They always want more."

In a loud voice, he proclaimed, "Gold it will be, then! You shall have your twenty-four-carat wish. Go back to your palace, Midas, and when you cross the threshold, you shall have the golden touch."

I was so excited, I ran all the way home. One of my sandals snagged and broke on the underbrush, but I was in such a hurry, I didn't stop to pick it up. When I finally got to the palace and stepped through the front door, my bare foot left a gold footprint on the marble floor.

I jumped up and down on one foot, making gold tracks all over the hall. Then, giggling wildly, I ran from room to room, running my fingers over everything—the walls, mirrors, tables, pillows, goblets. And everything I touched instantly changed to gold.

In the library I touched book after book, changing them

all into solid blocks of gold. Of course, I'd never be able to read them again, but what did I care? I didn't need wisdom or learning. Soon I would be the richest man in the world!

For hours I touched this thing and that, gilding the downstairs rooms of the palace until they were blindingly bright. Then, exhausted, I sat down on my most comfortable throne to rest. The moment my backside touched the cushion, it turned to gold. It was like sitting on a rock. A very *hard* rock.

I called for some food, and my retinue of servants came hurrying in, carrying steaming platters (cheap silver, I suddenly noticed). The smell was delicious. But no sooner had I put the first bite into my mouth than it turned to a tasteless lump of gold. The wine, too, thickened into gold sludge so that I choked on the first sip.

Dora, my beloved golden retriever, must have smelled the food. She bounded into the room and, before I could say "Sit!," jumped up, put her paws on my chest, and knocked me off my throne. I lay on the floor, the wind knocked out of me, a *real* gold retriever standing stiffly on my chest.

Then I heard my daughter's footsteps in the hall. "Papa?" she called. "Is that you?"

Terrified at what might happen next, I looked wildly around the room for another exit. Then I dove out the window, straight into the moat. Luckily, the spell didn't work outside the castle. If it had, I might have been swallowed up in a solid gold moat forever.

I swam the moat in record time and ran into the forest to

find Bacchus. When I did, I clung to his robes and implored him to take away what I had wished for.

"Tired of it all so soon, Midas?" he teased. "That was a quick cure." Then, with an amused smile, he told me to wash myself in the river Pactolus and all would be well. And when I did, the water turned gold around me, as if I were washing buckets of gold dust out of my clothes.

By the time I got back to the palace, everything was normal again. Books, carpets, mirrors, pillows, walls, floor—everything was just as it had been. Dora was waiting for me, rambunctious as ever. She jumped up and licked me, and then I saw that her *teeth* were still solid gold!

I don't know why . . . unless perhaps the gods wanted me to have a permanent reminder of my folly.

Unfortunately, my wish for the golden touch wasn't the only stupid thing I've done in my life. Soon after that, I was asked to be one of the judges for a musical contest between Apollo and Pan.

Apollo played an edifying hymn on his golden lyre, praising all the gods on Mt. Olympus, including himself. It was beautiful, but went on for what seemed forever. When Pan's turn came, he took out his homemade flute and played a rustic ditty about earthly matters—wine, romance, and song. To my ears, his music sounded like a merry little brook bubbling along.

I honestly liked Pan's song better, but the other judges disagreed and gave the prize to Apollo.

Apollo was enraged at how I'd voted. "Midas, you

fool, you dare to say a satyr plays better than I do!" he thundered.

Too late, I realized my mistake. Gods simply can't tolerate second place.

"Well," I squeaked, "perhaps it was a tie—"

"Only a tin-eared ass would say such a thing, so for the rest of your life, you shall have ass's ears."

That night my poor ears grew and grew, until, by morning, they were a foot long. I hid them under a silly-looking hat, tall and pointed like a dunce cap. Then I walked into court as if nothing had happened. Since I was king, my fawning courtiers made no mention of my strange appearance. In fact, they made my choice in hats the fashion. Soon everyone was strutting around the palace in tall, peaked caps that made them look like idiots.

My barber SWORE he'd never tell a soul about my ears. But after a few short weeks, the secret was too much for him. One day, bursting to tell somebody, the poor fellow ran out into an open field, miles from anywhere, dug a hole in the ground, and shouted into it, "*King Midas has ass's ears.*"

Relieved of his secret, he felt much better, but eventually a tuft of grass sprang up, and when the wind blew, it told my secret to every passing traveler:

> *King Midas has ass's ears,*
> *ass's ears, ass's ears . . .*
> *King Midas has ass's ears,*
> *ass's ears, ass's ears . . .*

One by one, each blade of grass took up the song, until the news spread to all four corners of my kingdom.

That taught me a lesson. Believe me, I'm a humbler man now. I spend most of my time puttering around in my rose garden. I no longer want wealth or fame. And when anyone asks which is better—a real rose or a solid gold one—I say I'll take a sweet red rose over the twenty-four-carat kind any day . . .

PAN AND SYRINX

LA-LA-LA-LA-LA, *La-la-la-la-la!* Do you like my flute? Some say my music is sweeter than Apollo's. I'm Pan, guardian of shepherds, goatherds, and beekeepers. Although I'm a god, I prefer earth to Mt. Olympus. Let me tell you why . . .

My father was Hermes, and some say my mother was Amalthea, the goat. I'm the unfortunate result. I was born with a beard and horns, a tail, and a goat's bandy legs. My father was so amused he carried me up to Olympus to show to the other gods.

Zeus took one look at me and, laughing, said, "Hermes, that son of yours looks like the very devil!"

"My goodness, he's ugly!" roared Apollo. "Was his mother a goat?" And all the gods and goddesses broke out in laughter.

Well, rather than be the laughingstock of Olympus, I decided to live on earth. I found a quiet little grotto in the mountains of Arcadia where I can sleep all day. If anyone dares to wake me up, I scream so loudly—a *panic*, they call it—that the intruder runs away in fright.

At night I make merry with wine and music. Some of the mountain nymphs like it, and some don't. I remember a shy one named Pitys who changed herself into a fir tree rather than spend time with me. I made one of her branches into a wreath to remember her by.

And then there was Syrinx. Ah, Syrinx! She was as beautiful as her name, but would have nothing to do with me. The only time I saw Syrinx, she had just come back from the hunt. She was sweating and out of breath, her clothes were in disarray, and her cheeks flushed, but I didn't mind.

I admit I'm not the subtle sort. I grabbed her around the waist and said, "Syrinx, let's get married!"

"You oaf," she cried. "Get away from me!" Then she gave me a push and began to run. Oh, how she could run! She was fleet as a deer, and I wondered if I'd be able to catch her. Then I saw the river ahead and knew luck was on my side.

Closer, I drew closer . . . I was one step behind when, at the river's edge, Syrinx paused, breathless, and called out to the water nymphs:

"Sisters, by the heavens above, deliver me from Pan!"

I threw my arms around her, but Syrinx was gone. Where she had stood, a tuft of reeds swayed on the riverbank, like a chorus of dancers. Syrinx was among them.

They made a soft singing sound in the rushing wind. Which gave me an idea.

I cut a handful, from short to long, tied them together, and made the first flute. "My Syrinx," I call it.

And so, though Syrinx escaped me, I have made her mine forever. I put my lips to her and make music sweet as the nightingale's.

Listen, and I'll play some scales for you.

do.   *Do*

ti   *ti*

la   *la*

so   *so*

fa   *fa*

mi   *mi*

re   *re*

Do   *do*

Have you ever heard anything sweeter?

PERSEPHONE AND DEMETER

I AM PERSEPHONE, the only daughter of Demeter, the goddess of the harvest. Together, we use our talents to make the earth bloom. I love spring best, and my gentle mother loves the fall. Everyone on earth knows her as the Good Goddess. All summer she watches over the fields of ripening grain. Come fall, she blesses the harvest so that there will be enough for everyone.

For the want of a flower, our happy life together came to an end. It happened like this. One spring day, I was playing with the wood nymphs in the vale of Enna when I saw a purple flower I had never seen before. Curious, I strayed too far from my companions so I could pick the black narcissus.

Suddenly the ground opened up, and Pluto, lord of the underworld, appeared in his black chariot, drawn by a team of sweating, coal-black horses. They pawed the ground, reared up, and snorted madly.

I screamed, and in a second Pluto had snatched me up,

turned his horses around, and was heading down to his king-dom in the underworld.

When we arrived at his palace, he said, "Persephone, I've brought you here to be my wife and queen—"

"Against my will!" I answered angrily.

"I'm sure it's a shock, but perhaps you will grow to like it here. Look around you. Everything that's mine is yours now, too, my dear."

He brought out onyx chests filled with gold and jew-els—diamonds, rubies, emeralds—but I said proudly, "My mother and I love the earth's bounty, its bright flowers, sweet fruit, and golden grain. What use have I for glittering jewels?"

"Well then," said Pluto with a sigh, "let me show you my garden. Perhaps *that* will meet your approval."

He steered me out into the terrible twilight. His gar-den was a silent, gloomy place. Willows, bent like weeping women, grew next to a stagnant pool. Everything was clipped and orderly and well tended, but none of it seemed *alive*.

"Are there no fruits or flowers here?" I cried. "No birds or bees? No butterflies?"

Pluto thought for a minute. "Well, I do have a pomegran-ate tree." He led me to a clearing where one blood-red pome-granate hung glistening on a branch of a small fruit tree.

"Won't you have a taste?" asked Pluto.

"I'd rather starve," I said. "I'll eat nothing until you agree to let me leave this place and go back to my mother."

But Pluto shook his head. He pointed to a marble throne, black, of course, and terribly uncomfortable. As queen of the underworld, I had to sit there with Pluto each day as arriving souls, newly dead, came to the palace to pay their respects.

Everyone told the same story. Above, on earth, my mother's grief at the loss of her daughter was so great that all of Nature grieved. The trees were bare, the earth covered with a heavy mantle of snow and ice. Nothing would grow, and in all the villages and towns, the people were slowly starving. My once beautiful mother, in the brief time I had been gone, had become gray and bent like an old woman.

"Please," I begged Pluto, "by heaven and earth's bounty, let me go!"

But Pluto stubbornly refused. Nothing would change his mind, until Hermes, Zeus' messenger, paid him a visit. It seemed the other gods and goddesses couldn't bear to see my mother suffer so. They had gone to Zeus and begged him to do something.

"Pluto," Hermes said, "you must give Persephone back to Demeter. If you don't, the human race will die out. Listen to reason, fellow! We can't have a heaven and an underworld without mortals. Who would admire us? Who would tell our stories? Who would we trifle with? And," he added, "if the human race comes to an end, you'll go out of business."

"And why is that?" asked Pluto.

"*No new souls to take in!*" answered Hermes in a booming voice. Then they fell to whispering.

The next day Pluto came to me. "Persephone," he began, "I know that you're unhappy here, so I've decided to send you back to your mother." He paused. "But I wouldn't want you to make the trip on an empty stomach. Your mother might think I've been starving you.

"So here," he coaxed. "Just a few bites of this pomegranate and you can be on your way." He held out the ripe red globe, and eager to return to earth, I quickly swallowed a few bites, seeds and all.

Then, in a whirling instant, I was back on earth, standing in the same meadow where I had been carried off. In the distance I saw my mother running toward me. Before my eyes she changed from an old gray-haired woman into a young, radiant goddess again. The snow melted and flowers sprang up in her footsteps. Trees put out pale green leaves. All over earth, glad sowers once again scattered seeds in the rich dark fields. It was spring!

We talked of all that had happened, oh how we talked, but then a shadow crossed her face. Fearfully, she asked, "Persephone, you didn't eat anything while you were in the underworld, I hope?"

"Only a few bites of a pomegranate," I confessed. "Pluto insisted. He said I shouldn't make the trip on an empty stomach."

"That scoundrel!" my mother cried. "Now Pluto has a claim on you. You see, he made a bargain with Zeus. For each pomegranate seed that you swallowed, you'll have to spend a month each year with him."

And so, through Pluto's trickery, I spend three months of the year in the underworld, one for each seed that I swallowed. And while I'm there, my mother grieves so terribly that snow and ice cover the earth and nothing grows. But every spring, I return to her, and the earth—fruits, flowers, grain—comes back to life.

Yes, I shall always come back. But I am not the carefree girl I once was. Now, like everyone on earth, I know sorrow as well as joy. I see how brief each season's beauty is. Even so, I give thanks that every spring, summer, and fall my mother and I will be together again.

SISYPHUS

JUST . . . GIVE . . . ME . . . A . . . MOMENT . . . and . . . I'll . . . tell . . . you . . . why . . . I'm . . . here . . . in . . . the . . . underworld . . . pushing . . . a . . . rock . . . as . . . big . . . as . . . an . . . elephant . . . up . . . this . . . stupid . . . hill . . .

Ahhh . . . I've . . . almost . . . got . . . it . . . to . . . the . . . top . . .

OH NO! There it goes again, down, down, down, to the bottom of the hill. Now I'll have to start all over again! You see, here in hell, we each have a job to do. There's no rest, no sleep, for the poor souls like me who live here. Just the same senseless task to do over and over and over.

But perhaps, if I talk fast, I can tell you why I'm here before Pluto puts me back to work. My name is Sisyphus. Once, I was King of Corinth. My father was Aeolus, guardian of the winds, which probably accounts for why I've always been able to talk my way out of any situation. Until now, that is . . .

My troubles started when Zeus abducted Aegina, the daughter of the river god Asopus. When Asopus came to Corinth looking for his daughter, I struck a bargain. I'd tell Asopus which way Zeus and Aegina had gone if he'd give my city a spring.

Asopus was stingy with his water, but he agreed. With his staff, he struck the ground, and fresh water bubbled up from an underground spring. I pointed him in the right direction, and he rushed off to find Zeus and Aegina.

Well, Zeus saw Asopus coming. Quickly he changed himself into a rock, and Aegina into a beautiful island. (You can still see her on a map, a blue jewel floating in the Mediterranean.) Zeus had to stay that way for hours, until Asopus finally gave up his search and went home.

When Zeus had taken his own form again, he was stiff, sore, and furious. He knew that I had betrayed him. So he asked his brother Pluto to take me down to the underworld and punish me for meddling in his affairs.

Pluto showed up at my door in his dark, gloomy robes, solemn as an undertaker. I swear, the man never smiled! He was carrying a pair of rusty old leg irons.

"Your time's up, Sisyphus," he announced with a yawn. "Now come along quietly, or I'll have to put you in these leg irons."

"Leg irons?" I asked, wide-eyed. "For a king? They look a little rusty. Are you sure they work?"

Pluto bent down and snapped them shut and open with a key. I asked if I could try. In the wink of an eye, the key was in my hand and Pluto was chained by his ankle to my door-post!

"Hey, turn me loose!" shouted Pluto angrily. But I wouldn't hand over the key. And that caused a lot of trouble in the world. As long as Pluto was my prisoner, no one could die. Not hanged men, not people who had drowned, not even one poor fellow who had just been beheaded. Everyone on the brink of death simply had to wait . . . and wait . . . and wait.

The Three Fates, who usually control such things, started quarreling. They tangled life's threads as if they were fishing lines.

Finally Ares, the god of war, descended on the palace, boiling mad. Of course, once he had set Pluto free, the first person to die was me. But I had another trick up my sleeve. As I was leaving, I whispered to my wife, Merope, *not* to bury me or give me any sort of funeral.

"No coin under my tongue either," I added, winking.

When I arrived in the underworld, I had no money to pay Charon, the ferryman who takes dead souls across the river Styx. The fare was one coin—copper, silver, or gold, depending on your rank in life. But I didn't have even a penny.

"This is most irregular," said Charon. "You were a king, and yet you've come to the underworld like a beggar."

"Oh, PLEASE, PLEASE, PLEASE, let me cross," I whined in a loud voice, as if I were dying to get into hell. (I really was hoping to attract the attention of Persephone, Pluto's unhappy queen, whose palace window had a river view.)

"Sorry, no coin, no ride," Charon said. "That's the policy."

Sure enough, Persephone heard the ruckus and came out of the palace to intervene.

"Charon, what's wrong here?" she asked.

"This fellow doesn't have the fare—" Charon rudely began, but I interrupted him.

"Your Highness," I explained, wiping a tear from my eye, "I've barely been dead a day and already my wife has forgotten me. She didn't bother with a funeral or give me a coin for the passage here. Could I have your leave to return to earth and straighten things out?"

"He's a simple crook!" sputtered Charon, but Persephone felt sorry for me. (She'd always hated living in the underworld.) She let me go back to earth to teach my wife the proper way of doing things.

And so I spun out my life with Merope for a while longer. Of course, there came a time when Pluto refused to be put off. This time he brought a ball and chain, and his dog Cerberus, an awful-looking mutt with three heads. He wasn't taking any chances the second time around.

I took one look at that dog and went down to the underworld meek as a lamb.

Once we got there, Pluto smiled and said, "Sisyphus, I've come up with the perfect punishment for you. You see that rock?"

He pointed to a boulder that looked a lot like the one Zeus had turned himself into.

"I want you to push it to the top of that hill. And if, by chance, it rolls back down—which I assure you it will—then

PUSH IT TO THE TOP AGAIN!!!

Understand?"

I nodded. Sometimes it's best to cooperate, especially when a three-headed dog is snapping at your heels.

So here I am. From the top of the hill, I can see the Elysian Fields, where all the heroes, like Hercules and Orion, get to live. It's beautiful over there. The grass is green, the music sweet, and the wine never runs out. In a century or two, when Zeus' anger dies down, I'm going to ask for a transfer—

Oh no, here come Pluto and Cerberus. I'd better get back to work!

One . . . day . . . I'll . . . get . . . this . . . rock . . . to . . . the . . . top . . . of . . . the . . . hill . . . or . . . my . . . name . . . isn't . . . Sisyphus . . .

I will, I tell you! I will!

NARCISSUS AND ECHO

OH ME, OH MY, another boring day in the underworld! Which mirror shall I look in first today? The big one there on the wall? Or the small one here on the table? The tiny one I wear as a pendant around my neck? Or the pocket mirror I carry with me everywhere?

And after I admire myself for a while, then what shall I do?

Perhaps I'll paint another self-portrait . . . but if I *do* paint myself, what pose should I choose? Should I recline on the chaise longue? Or draw myself in profile? Should I smile? Or look thoughtful? Decisions, decisions, there are so many decisions to make, and yet every day is the same here. Thank goodness, I have my mirrors. I'd be bored stiff without them.

You must be wondering what I'm doing here. I'm young, I'm handsome, so why come down to hell prematurely?

It's a fascinating story, really, and one I never tire of

telling (because it's about *me*). It began when I was a boy. I was so handsome that every girl I met fell madly in love with me. By the time I was sixteen, I had broken hundreds of hearts.

Yes, all the nymphs adored me, especially one named Echo. Echo was the most lovesick girl I've ever known. Night and day, she followed me everywhere, hiding behind rocks and trees, gazing at me like a lovesick cow. She rarely said a word; in fact, she *couldn't* speak unless someone spoke to her first.

It was all Hera's fault. And Zeus', too. They had the worst marriage in the universe, and Zeus always had a secret girlfriend or two. One day he decided to have a private picnic with the nymphs. Afraid that Hera might find out and cause a scene, Zeus told Echo to distract Hera for as long as she could.

When Hera appeared, looking for Zeus as usual, Echo ran up to her and began chattering nonstop. For half an hour Echo talked and talked and talked! Finally Hera, suspecting a trick, said, "Enough!" and, pointing a finger, sealed Echo's lips.

"From now on, my girl," Hera said, "you'll say nothing unless you're spoken to. And when you do speak, you'll mirror what you hear. You'll say only what others say. No more."

"—*say only what others say? No more?*" repeated Echo stupidly.

Poor Echo! After that, she was usually mute as a stone.

But that didn't stop her from following me everywhere. Finally, I couldn't stand the sight of her.

"Go away!" I told her. "I don't want you to follow me!"

"*Follow me!*" she begged, and pitifully held out her arms.

"No!" I said. "Listen to me, you brainless girl, I do not love you. Do not love me!"

"*You do not love me?*" she asked, her eyes wet with tears.

"That's right," I repeated coldly. "I do not love you. So do not love me."

"*Love me,*" she senselessly begged.

And so it went. Talking to Echo was hopeless. But the other nymphs thought I was heartless. They said I'd treated Echo badly. (Truth to tell, they were fed up with my conceited ways themselves.) They prayed to Artemis that I— like Echo—would fall in love with someone who would never love me back.

Soon after, I came upon a pool in the forest that I had never noticed before. It was clear and smooth as poured silver. When I knelt to drink, the water shimmered like a looking glass. And in the water I saw a boy, a beautiful boy, looking up at me, his eyes wide with longing and surprise.

In a heartbeat, I fell in love with a perfect stranger.

"Do you love me?" I asked. The boy stared at me. His lips moved, but he made no sound.

"Kiss me!" I begged. When the boy did nothing, I bent to kiss him, but the minute my lips touched the water, he melted away. I waited for the water to clear, and there he was again, wide-eyed and waiting.

But each time I plunged my arms in the pool, hoping to haul him out, he disappeared. So I sat there, miserable, knowing for the first time what it was like to be love's prisoner.

Weeks passed that way, with me rooted to the spot. Instead of my infatuation passing, I only desired the beautiful stranger more and more. I couldn't eat or sleep, and gradually began to pine away. I lost weight, and my skin took on a deathly pallor. When I was just a pale shade of myself—but still handsome!—Hermes led me down to the underworld.

On the ferry ride across the river Styx, I looked over the boat railing and sighed. The boy in the pool had followed me! There he was in the dark water, looking up at me, longing in his eyes. He *did* love me.

"Farewell," I said, as I stepped off the ferry. Faintly I heard a reply, "Farewell," but it was only lovesick Echo on the far shore making a mockery of my love.

Pluto was waiting for me. He looked at me and shook his head in disgust.

"So you're Narcissus," he said. "I've heard all about you. The gods in heaven told me you're a hopeless case. We'll see about that.

"Normally," Pluto went on, "I'm here to punish souls. I take away their pleasures and give them horrible, senseless jobs to do. But in your case, I have something a little different planned. I want you to take these"—he pointed to a pile of glittering mirrors stacked haphazardly next to his throne—"and decorate your room here any way that you please."

"That's all?" I asked, surprised. "No shirts of flame? No unquenchable thirst or gnawing hunger? No stones to endlessly roll up a hill?"

"Narcissus," said Pluto, "this is the modern age! We're moving beyond simple medieval torture into something more up-to-date. I think what we have planned for you is more than adequate. Now go. And make sure you take *all* the mirrors."

"Thanks!" I said, and thought to myself how generous Pluto was.

In my room I hung the mirrors everywhere—on all four walls and even on the ceiling. Then I lay back in a chaise longue Pluto had thoughtfully provided. I looked up at my reflection on the ceiling and thought to myself, *Narcissus, you really are a handsome fellow!*

For several days my situation seemed ideal. I couldn't understand the gruesome tales I'd heard about the underworld.

And then it began . . . the echo. At first, it was just occasionally—

Narcissus, I love you, love you, love you . . .

—but, lately, I hear it night and day. Could Echo have followed me here?

Narcissus, I love you, love you, love you . . .

Narcissus, I love you, love you, love you . . .

Over and over and over! Despite the commendable sentiments, I'm ready for a break. It's like the *drip, drip, drip* of a leaky faucet, or the endless, maddening *tick, tock, tick* of a clock.

Narcissus, I love you, love you, love you . . .

Narcissus, I love you, love you, love you . . .

Narcissus, I love you, love you, love you . . .

I tell you, my head is ringing. There it is again! Can you hear it? It seems to be getting louder.

Narcissus, I love you, love you, love you . . .

Narcissus, I love you, love you, love you . . .

Narcissus, I love you, love you, love you . . .

Narcissus, I love you, love you, love you . . .

Whenever I complain to Pluto about it, he just smiles and tells me it's all in my imagination. He pats me on the shoulder, says, "Poor boy!" and walks off unconcerned.

If it doesn't stop soon, I'll go mad. I'm exhausted, I can't sleep, and today in the mirror I saw the worst thing I've ever seen in my life—

My face with a wrinkle on it!

TITHONUS

CHREEEP, *chreeep! Chreeep, chreeep!*

Pssst! I'm over here, in this basket. But don't open the lid. Not yet. Just put your ear close and I'll tell you about the time I was prince.

It happened like this: One morning, after a late night out, I was fast asleep in the palace. The shutters were closed tightly against the dawn, so imagine my surprise when the room began to fill with a soft pink light. Then I felt a girl's fingers gently stroking my hair. I opened my eyes, and there was Aurora, goddess of the dawn, gazing at me with lovesick eyes.

I thought I was dreaming, but no, I touched her and she was real, as real as you are.

"Tithonus," she sighed, "you are the handsomest man alive. Marry me, or I know I shall perish from this love."

I was willing, but worried. I knew these matches between mortals and immortals usually came to a bad end.

"Aurora," I began, "I would marry you but for one thing. Someday I'll be a wrinkled old man hobbling around with a cane and you'll still be young and beautiful. It preys on my mind that you wouldn't love me then."

"Never mind that. I've taken care of everything," she said, with a careless wave of her hand. "I went to Zeus and asked him to make you immortal. He said yes. If that's all that troubles you, we can be married today."

And so we were. We lived in Aurora's palace, a little east of where the sun rises, a marvelous affair of pink-and-blue marble. Every morning Aurora woke, fresh as a rosebud (the mornings were her favorite time), and gave me a kiss. The years passed like weeks, we were that happy.

But after a while, I began to slow down. And when it rained, my bones ached as if I had rheumatism!

Then one day I noticed that all the mirrors in the palace were gone.

"Aurora," I called, "where is that mirror I like to look in?"

"Why, Tithonus, I have no idea," she said, looking frightened, as if she had something to hide. "Perhaps the serving girl mislaid it." Then she tried to change the subject.

This went on for several days. When I finally found the mirror hidden under a pile of linens, I looked into it and was shocked to see . . . a gray hair.

"Aurora," I cried, "what is this? My youth is gone! I thought you said Zeus made me immortal?"

Aurora began to weep. "Oh, Tithonus, forgive me. I made

a terrible mistake. I forgot to ask Zeus to give you eternal youth as well as eternal life. You *will* live forever, but I'm afraid you may get a gray hair or two. But don't worry. I'll love you till the end of time, gray hairs or not."

And for a while Aurora kept her word. She was more devoted than ever. She took care of me as if I were her father . . . or grandfather. I grew stooped and walked with a cane. Aurora helped me up the steps, and when my hand shook, she fed me with a spoon.

By the time I was eighty, I was bent as a question mark. And with each passing decade, I was reduced still more. By the time I was a hundred, my arms and legs were thin as matchsticks. I was frail as a robin!

"Aurora, my love," I wheezed and rasped, "could you shut the window? I feel a terrible draft. And when you get a chance, could you bring me my lap robe? I can't find it anywhere. Oh, and one more thing, a glass of warm milk might be nice."

"Tithonus," she said irritably, "looking after you is a full-time job. You are no more than a husk of a man. Why, the wind might blow you away! What am I to do?"

And so, to keep me safe, Aurora put me in this basket.

At first I protested. It seemed an extreme thing to do. But I've grown to like it well enough. It's dark in here but comfortable. Do you want to see? Well, open the lid, but only a little. The light hurts my eyes.

There, can you see me now? Yes, back here in the shadows. It's me, Tithonus, shrunk to the size of a grasshopper.

Funny, isn't it, what the years will do? Well, one good thing has come out of all this. I'm now an accomplished musician. To prove it, I'll play you a tune.

Chreeep! Chreeep!

Chreeepity-chreeepity-chreeep!

Chreeep! Chreeep!

Chreeepity-chreeepity-chreeep!

Chreeep!

ENDYMION AND SELENE

I AM SELENE. You know me as the moon. Each night I drive my white mares silently across the sky, lighting the dreaming world below. Joy, pain, sorrow: I see everything that goes on—children being born, couples falling in love, soldiers going off to war, old men and women dying.

For thousands of years I didn't get involved in earthly matters. But it isn't easy being the moon. It's lonely up here, so cold and so black, with only the stars for company. And I'm changeable. I wax and I wane, and sometimes I disappear completely, but I always come back. I have to. I'm the moon and the human world needs me.

Like my sister Aurora, I fell in love with a mortal, a beautiful shepherd named Endymion. Driving my team one night, I spied him sleeping on Mt. Latmos, his flocks untended, scattered like bits of cotton wool up and down the hillside.

I drove on, but couldn't get him out of my mind. The

next night I reined in my horses and came down to earth. All night long I sat beside him. Gently I stroked his cheek.

"Endymion," I whispered, "It is Selene, come to you in the fullness of love." But he didn't stir. Alive, breathing, warm, he only smiled in his sleep. That smile undid me.

I kissed him—once, twice, three times!—but nothing could wake him from the dream he was dreaming.

At dawn I had to leave, of course. I began to pine away to nothing. When Zeus asked me what was wrong, I confessed that I loved Endymion.

"You?" said Zeus, surprised. "Cold Selene in love with a mortal?"

I nodded, embarrassed. Then I begged Zeus to grant Endymion eternal youth *and* eternal sleep, so that I could spend all my nights with him.

Zeus granted my wish. Perhaps it was selfish what I asked, but at least I didn't make the same mistake as Aurora. Till the end of time, she'll have a noisy old grasshopper for a husband while I'll have one handsome and young.

Years have passed, so many years. We have fifty daughters, pale and sleepy-eyed like their father, their skin white as cream. They circle Endymion like little moons, they tug at his hands and softly sing, "*Father, wake up and play with us. Wake up!*" But Endymion sleeps on.

Sometimes now, I feel a human pain, the pain of loving someone who can't love back. Endymion, if only you would open your eyes! But you can't, you can't, any more than I can stop shining.

Look! He is smiling again. Oh, what does that smile mean? Is he dreaming he holds me in his arms?

Endymion, I know one thing: If you *did* wake up, I wouldn't kiss you. Oh no. After fifty daughters, I've had enough kissing to last me ten lifetimes.

Instead, I'd like to talk to you. Just talk!

CALLISTO

LOOK UP and you'll see me, *there*, in the night sky. But I'm getting ahead of my story . . .

I was a maiden in Artemis' hunting party when Zeus picked me out and declared his love. We had a son, Arcas, but when Zeus' wife, Hera, found out, she flew into a rage. Of course, she blamed me for everything.

Arcas was only a newborn when Hera appeared, cool and furious, and said with a cruel smile:

"Never again, you brazen girl, will you smile into a mirror, sing a sweet song, or run swiftly on two legs. From this day on, you shall live in speechless terror in a dismal wood. From maiden into beast, from hunter into hunted, that is your punishment for stealing Zeus."

"But Zeus is to blame—" I began, which only made Hera more furious. Even as I spoke, my slender hands grew round and blunt and clawed. Dark fur sprouted on my face and arms, and without warning, I dropped down on all fours. I opened my mouth to scream, but all that came out was a deep groan.

Hera had changed me into a bear.

And all that Hera said came true. Alone, I roamed the dark forest remembering, in pain, how I had once been human. I lost count of the years. I lived in fear of hunters, desperately missed my son, and wished that Zeus would appear. But Zeus did nothing. He rarely interfered in Hera's affairs.

And then one day I heard dogs and hunters returning from the hunt. There, in the distance, I saw my son, a young man now! Forgetting what I was, I ran to embrace him. I stood up on my hind legs to touch him tenderly, but Arcas brandished his spear and certainly would have killed me if Zeus, at that very moment, hadn't appeared. He stayed my son's hand and declared for all to hear:

"Callisto, you have suffered greatly. I place you now beyond the reach of Hera's wrath. Never again shall you and Arcas be parted. Mother and son, the two of you shall shine in the heavens as the Great Bear and the Little Bear."

And with those words, Zeus snatched us up and set us among the stars.

At that, Hera flew into another rage. She rushed to Oceanus, the Titan who ruled the seas, and rudely demanded a favor.

"Zeus has gone behind my back again!" she screamed. "I changed that scheming girl Callisto into a bear—exactly what she deserved! Now Zeus gives her a place of honor among the stars. If you would side with me, I ask that you forbid Callisto and her son to set foot in your seas. While other constellations rise and set freely, I desire that Callisto and Arcas circle the northern pole star forever without relief."

Oceanus, of course, agreed. What else could he do? He didn't dare cross Hera, even if he wanted to.

And so, on any clear night, winter or summer, you can see the two of us—Ursa Major and Ursa Minor—*there*, in the northern regions, circling round and round Polaris.

We look down on a world as troubled as when we left it. But for as long as Time lasts, we are safe here, removed forever from human pain and unhappiness . . .

CLYTIE

LISTEN TO MY STORY and tell me if love is kind or unkind. Once I was happy, a nymph playing with my sisters by the river . . .

Then Apollo rode by in his golden chariot, blinding me with his smile. My wise sisters looked away, but I drank in Apollo's flashing hair and eyes and fell in love.

How I wanted Apollo to notice me! But I did not shout, "Apollo! Look at me! Only at me!"

Instead, that evening I devised a plan. At dawn, on the hill above the river, I would wait for Apollo. In a dress golden as the sun, I would swear eternal love.

And so, at break of day, I planted myself on the hilltop. And just as I had hoped, Apollo's chariot rose up from the east and came thundering toward me. But he did not stop! Apollo paid no more attention to me than to a blade of grass.

He rushed across the sky, dragging the hours with him, and was gone.

The next day was the same. And the next. The other nymphs surrounded me and begged, "Sister, forget this foolish attraction! Apollo does not love you. Come back to the river with us."

But I turned away, deaf as a stone. My heart was set on Apollo. Tomorrow he would notice me. Tomorrow.

For nine days I waited. Nights, I shivered in my fine dress, too thin to keep me warm. When the wind blew, my tangled hair streamed around me. I was a sight! I hardly slept and had no appetite. Thirsty, I tasted my own tears and drank the chilly dew.

And every day Apollo ignored me. Like a foolish spendthrift, he scattered his precious light on everything—bird, beast, and flower—but never on me alone. But still I craned my neck from east to west, following his every move.

My sisters grew impatient. They scolded, "You foolish, stubborn girl! Stop this nonsense! Come back to the river with us before it is too late!"

But on the ninth day they looked at me, amazed, and only said, "Sister, a great change has come over you. We hope it is for the best." And off they went, shaking their heads.

Yes, it is true, I am not myself today. My head is large and heavy, my hair plaited in ragged gold strands. My neck has a dreadful pain in it from twisting this way and that.

And my beautiful dress . . . where is it? The wind must have blown it away.

Apollo, day after day, I have stared at you like a slave. To what purpose? When will you carry me away?

Who speaks to you? It is I, poor Clytie, changed into a sunflower.

SHE LOVES ME. She loves me not. She loves me. She loves me not. She loves me. She loves me not. Ah! This daisy says she loves me!

Yes, that's right. Pomona loves me! But it wasn't always so. For a long time Pomona cared only about her orchards and vineyards. While all the other wood nymphs happily played in the forest, Pomona's joy was her fruit trees and grapevines. From dawn to dusk, she clipped and pruned with a passion, but had no time for men. She swore she'd never marry and even built a high stone wall around her property to keep everyone out!

But suitors hounded her anyway. You should have seen them, big bragging boys that weren't her type at all, fauns, satyrs, and other minor deities, including Pan. Day after day, they stood outside Pomona's gate, each claiming to be the strongest, the bravest, the most handsome. But I stood back from the fray watching as Pomona told them all to go away.

"Men!" she scolded. "Men are in love with love! But marriage takes more work and bears less fruit than the scrawniest fruit tree ever will. I'd rather be changed into a tree like Daphne than marry you or you or you!"

And with that, she turned on her heel and left them all standing there.

One by one, everyone gave up, except for me. I had only one thought: How could I win Pomona? How?

Then I had an idea. I went back to my house and put on a big straw hat and a reaper's rough shirt and pants. I grabbed a basket of barley ears and showed up barefoot at Pomona's gate.

"Barley ears! Barley ears! All for you! And a willing pair of hands to do whatever you want me to!" I gaily sang.

Perched high on a ladder, Pomona was pruning one of her apple trees. She looked down at me as if I were an ant, then waved me away, saying, "I have enough barley ears in my storeroom to last me ten years. And help is the last thing I need from a man. Goodbye, whoever you are, and don't come back!"

And that, she thought, was the end of that.

But the next day there I was again, dressed in another rustic outfit, carrying sharp, shiny pruning shears almost as tall as I was. When I offered to prune her grapevines, Pomona shook her finger at me.

"You idiot!" she scolded. "Those shears are big enough to fell an oak! They're not for grapevines! You seem to know as much about vineyards as I know about astronomy. Now go away and stop bothering me."

Well, I've never been one to give up. Bright and early the next morning, I was back, this time in a shepherd's tunic and a big floppy hat.

Leaning on my shepherd's crook, I called:

"Shepherd for hire! Shepherd for hire! I'll tend your sheep for a few coins and my keep!"

Pomona opened the garden gate an inch and looked out at me in disbelief. "If you're a shepherd, I'm Cleopatra," she said. "Those creatures mooing on the hillside aren't sheep, you fool. They're cows!"

Squinting (I've always been a little nearsighted), I saw that she was right.

Pomona looked me up and down suspiciously and said, "Weren't you here yesterday? And the day before that? If you don't stop bothering me, I'm going to have you locked up!"

Then she slammed the gate in my face.

And so it went. I pretended to be a fisherman, a soldier, a jack-of-all-trades. I came with ladders and scythes and plows and offered to do odd jobs. But Pomona would never let me in.

So I went to the market in town and bought a dress and an old gray wig. I stuffed pillows in the dress until I looked as lumpy as a bowl of half-cooked oatmeal. I put on the wig, powdered my face, and rubbed rouge on my cheeks.

Then, leaning on my cane, I hobbled up to Pomona's gate.

"Oh dear, how hot it is today!" I exclaimed in a high voice, wiping my brow with a handkerchief. "And how my back aches! Can an old woman come in and rest for a moment in the shade? And perhaps sip a dipper of cold water from your well?"

For a change, Pomona smiled.

"Why, of course," Pomona said with a sweetness I hadn't heard before. "Come in and rest in my garden." She opened the gate, took me by the arm, and led me to a stone bench in the shade of an apple tree.

Then Pomona drew some water from the well in a silver dipper. Leaning over me, she smiled an innocent smile and gently held it to my lips. How sweet that water tasted coming from Pomona!

"What beautiful apples, my dear," I said, choosing my words with care. "So ripe and so red. But still, not half so beautiful as the hair on your own head."

At that very moment Pomona dropped the dipper—on purpose, or was it an accident?—and ice-cold water cascaded down my dress.

I jumped up, shouting, and took my chance. Quickly I kissed her on the lips!

Startled, Pomona blushed, her cheeks turning a delicious shade of red . . . just like the apples on her tree.

Before she could say anything, I gestured to a nearby grapevine, heavy with purple grapes, twining round and round the oak tree.

"Pomona, look how the grapevine clings to the oak. Without the oak, what would the vine do? It needs the tree to help it bear its fruit. And without the vine, the oak would simply be an oak. Together, heart to heart, they are so much more than they could ever be apart.

"Pomona," I went on, "there is one, a special one, who loves you as the rain loves the rose, as a fish loves the sea, as a bird loves the wind that carries it along. He is the one for you, Pomona. You know him. It is Vertumnus."

"NO!"—Pomona began—"I won't—"

My hand on her wrist, I stopped her.

"Pomona," I went on, looking into her eyes, "remember the story of Anaxarete? How, cruel girl that she was, she turned away her gentle suitor, Iphis? Remember how, distraught and brokenhearted, he took his life after Anaxarete refused to be his wife? Venus turned that heartless girl to stone. Pomona, do you, too, have a heart of stone? Don't live your life alone. Accept Vertumnus and he will give you everything, earth, moon, and sun."

And then, hot and sweating, I tore off my dress and wig and kissed her again!

And so, with words, beautiful words, and a kiss or two, I convinced Pomona to marry me. Now, side by side, we tend her orchards and vineyards together, and the harvest is twice what it was before.

Venus is happy, I'm happy, and even Pomona is happy. I don't tell Pomona everything I know about love, but I'll tell you.

Kisses speak louder than words!

CEYX AND HALCYONE

CEYX, who was happier than we were? You were King of Thessaly, the radiant son of Hesperus, the evening star. I was the daughter of Aeolus, keeper of the winds. We married and lived in perfect peace and harmony. Nothing came between us until, one day, you said you had to sail to Ionia to consult the oracle.

I felt a chill, a premonition. I knew what the sea could do to ships and men. As a girl in my father's windy palace, I'd watched the quarreling waves beat and batter passing ships. I'd seen men's lives shipwrecked by the storms.

Ceyx, remember how I begged you not to go? And when you said you had to, how I begged to go with you?

But you shook your head. I still remember your words: "Dear Halcyone, there is nothing to fear. In two months I'll be back. Let's hear no more about it."

Then you and your men raised the sails on your ship, and

with the help of my father, Aeolus, away you went, driven by a westerly wind. From the headlands I watched your ship grow smaller and smaller. Finally, no bigger than a tear, it reached the horizon and disappeared.

I went back to the palace, your promise echoing in my head: "*Two months, two months . . .*"

I prayed to the goddess Juno to protect you. I burned incense and made offerings. To pass the time, I wove two robes splendid as the day—one to lay on your shoulders the day of your homecoming and one that I would wear in bright gladness.

Two months passed. Then three. Then four. And still there was no sign of you. Each day I watched from the headlands, wanting to be the first to glimpse your ship's return. But the sea and sky were blank as a sheet of paper.

Finally I could take no more. Alone one day, white seabirds circling above me, I cried out, "Ceyx, where are you? Am I to wait forever for your return?" But my voice was drowned out by the unceasing wind.

That night Juno took pity on me. She asked Somnus, the god of sleep, to send me a dream. So Morpheus, Somnus' son, who can change his face and form to look like any man, flew through the dark air on wings and stood by my bed. He took your shape, Ceyx, so that, dreaming, I thought it was *you.*

Naked and wet, your beard soaked, seaweed tangled in your hair, you stood there, close enough to touch. But your face was white as death, your skin pocked and scarred with salt. You clasped my warm hand in your cold one and said:

"Beloved Halcyone, it is your husband, Ceyx. All that you feared has happened. My ship went down in a storm, dragging me and all my men to the bottom of the sea. Yes, we are all drowned. O Halcyone, I have walked the length of the sea floor to be with you once more. Weep your salt tears, dear one, so that I will not go down to Pluto's realm unmourned."

"No! Don't go! Wait for me!" I cried out in my sleep. A cry so loud it woke me. But you were gone, and I knew it was no dream. A pool of water, a single strand of seaweed lay on the stone floor where you had stood.

At dawn I rose and dressed myself. Like a sleepwalker, I went out to the headlands and numbly watched the waves crashing against the shore. And saw . . . What did I see?

Your body, Ceyx, floating in the waves, arms outstretched, drifting toward me. Closer, you floated closer, and I leaped without thinking off the cliff—to be with you! But I did not fall or drown. Instead, I rose on two white wings. I was flying! Flying!

Juno, in her mercy, had changed me into a bird. I swooped down to where you were. My wing touched your shoulder, and you, too, by Juno's grace, became a bird.

Now, two seabirds, we ride the waves side by side, we scale the updrafts into bright airy realms. And once each year, my father, Aeolus, calms the seas so that my nest of

eggs can float unharmed. See it there floating on the waves?
All will be perfect peace for seven days, the weather still and
shining.

These are the days that sailors wait and pray for. The halcyon days, they're called. May they always come back.

BAUCIS AND PHILEMON

WHO SHALL TELL OUR STORY, Philemon, you or I?

You tell it, Baucis, and I'll add to it as you go along.

Well, we had been married for how long, Philemon?

Oh, I'd say fifty years—

And we were poor but happy. Our cottage was one simple room. A cheerful place I swept each day with a twig broom to keep it clean. And I kept a fire going in the fireplace—

Yes, it always felt like home.

One day two travelers knocked at our door—an old man and his son—a handsome pair, although their clothes were dusty from the road. They said they were passing through Phrygia and asked if they could spend the night. They told us they had asked for lodging at every house in the village, and no one would invite them in.

They'd had doors slammed in their faces! So much for Phrygian hospitality.

Of course we told them they could stay with us. Our door is always open to strangers—

We trust in heaven to protect us.

It was suppertime when they knocked. I stretched the soup by adding a little water, and dropped in the last of the salt and bacon. And I set out radishes, cheese, and olives, and roasted a few eggs in the fire's ashes. That's all we had. For drink, we offered them some wine—

Not what you'd find on a king's table—

But they seemed well pleased. And then we noticed something strange. As fast as we poured the wine, the pitcher refilled itself. We filled their cups a second and a third time, and still the pitcher was as full as when we started! And that's when we suspected these weren't ordinary travelers—

—and so we decided we'd better catch and cook our goose to make it a real feast. No holding back in case these strangers happened to be gods!

Yes, we tried to catch the goose! Poor thing! We chased it, flapping, round and round the room, but it was faster than we were. Philemon, in his haste, tripped over a stool and went flying, and the goose settled in the old man's lap and wouldn't budge—

—as if it somehow knew the stranger would protect it.

Throughout the entire spectacle, our guests were quite amused—

Yes, they seemed to be enjoying themselves.

Laughing, they told us to leave the goose alone and sit down and finish our supper. Finally, when the table was cleared, we found out who they were. This is the part you won't believe—

Oh yes, they will!

They were Jupiter and Mercury! They'd disguised themselves as men and come down from heaven to test earthly hospitality. And we were the only ones in Phrygia who had welcomed them! Then Jupiter, remembering the rude villagers, raised his staff. We heard a terrible rush and roar, and when we looked outside, we saw he'd flooded the countryside.

Fortunately our house was on a hill—

—but all the houses in the village had been swept away. A lake, green and still as a jewel, extended as far as the eye could see. Then, in the time it takes to say this, our cottage disappeared. A marble temple with golden pediments stood shimmering in its place!

Then Jupiter said, "Good people, you shared what you had with us without a thought of blessing or reward. Now let us make your lives a little easier. Ask anything you wish and we will grant it."

Philomen and I thought for a minute, then asked if we could be the guardians of the temple—

—*and when our time on earth was over, if we could die together.*

And that's what happened. For years we happily took care of the temple, although it was never quite the home our cottage had been. There were so many rooms—

—*the place was always cold and drafty!*

Finally, when we were quite ancient, we knew our lives were coming to an end. We remembered the hard and happy times, and felt content with the life we'd had. As we clasped each other's hands, a sudden change came over us. Our feet took root in the ground, and by Jupiter's grace, we were changed into—

—two trees!

An oak and linden growing from the same trunk! Bark rushed up our bodies, covering our lips, eyes, hair. Our arms branched and leafed and twisted toward heaven, just as you see them now. So here we are, in a form that's different—

—and not so different—

—from what we were before. And travelers like yourself come to marvel at the marriage of two trees. They honor us by placing flowering wreaths in our branches.

Yes, all that we've said is true.

But, Philomen, tell me why today we said what we just said?

The wind, rushing through our leaves, wanted us to say it.

ORPHEUS AND EURYDICE

MT. OLYMPIAN
Poet Goes to Hell and Back

HADES DISPATCH
Stones Weep, Trees Bow Down at Poet's Grief

DAILY GODDESS
"Bring Me Back to Life!"
Begs Eurydice

HAVE YOU SEEN the evening newspapers? Yes, that's Orpheus they're talking about. He's famous now, the most famous poet on earth. And who am I? I'm Eurydice, his wife. I was married to Orpheus for about fifteen minutes when I was bitten by a poisonous snake and brought down to the underworld. So much for *my* happiness. But I'm getting ahead of my story . . .

My husband was the son of Calliope, one of the nine Muses. There was never any doubt he'd be a poet. When he was a boy, his mother and eight aunts—Clio, Erato, Euterpe, Melpomene, Polyhymnia, Terpsichore, Thalia, and Urania—simply doted on him. They sang him endless songs and lullabies, schooled him in poetry, and told him wonderful stories about how the gods created the world. Apollo took an interest in him, too, and gave him a tiny lyre to play.

Marvelous things happened when Orpheus played his lyre. Rivers changed their course, and trees and rocks moved closer to listen. Wild beasts lay purring at his feet, tame as housecats, and the songbirds in the forest fell silent in admiration.

Besides music, Orpheus loved poetry. He dashed off sonnets as easily as some people scribble down shopping lists. He wrote poems in the sand at the seashore and carved them into the trunks of trees.

Best of all, he wrote love poems. Truth to tell, some of them weren't very good, but I had a weakness for the ones about *me*:

> *Eurydice, without you,*
> *my lyre is liar,*
> *the songs I sing are wrong.*
> *I'm flat, off-key, as miserable as misery.*

> *Without you,*
> *I cannot hear the beat,*
> *I dance with two left feet,*
> *and have no appetite to eat.*

> *When we're apart,*
> *the stars are only stars,*
> *and words are only words,*
> *and nothing rhymes the way it ought.*

> *So, dearest, say yes to my proposal,*
> *and I will always be at your disposal!*

Of course I said yes when Orpheus asked me to marry him. But right after the wedding—we had it outdoors in a meadow—I was bitten by a viper, fainted dead away, and was carried down to the underworld by Hermes. When I woke up, Persephone, Pluto's unhappy wife, was bending over me with smelling salts.

"Poor child," she said. "So young to end up here! And just married, too! Well, in time you'll adjust. I have." She sighed, and I noticed dark circles under her eyes.

Up on earth, Orpheus was in a terrible state. Weeping and moaning, he wandered the hills and valleys of Thrace, playing songs so sad that all of Nature grieved with him. Clouds let loose great gusts of rain, the ocean churned in turmoil, and a bitter wind tore his clothes into rags.

Finally he resolved to do what no mortal had ever done—to come down to the underworld and beg for my return. At World's End, he found hell's entrance and, calming himself, stepped into the gloom. Down, down, down, he descended, playing his lyre and singing, the path pitch-dark and twisting. Like a silver line, his song went out ahead of him and led him safely on.

As Orpheus drew closer to Pluto's realm, Cerberus, hell's three-headed watchdog, stopped growling, whimpered softly, and licked his ankles like a puppy. The padlock on the underworld's great iron gates fell open, and inside, all of hell's torments stopped.

Sisyphus sat down on his rock to listen, and the great rock softened like a pillow.

Narcissus dropped his mirror.

Persephone's face lit up with joy.

A speechless shade, I watched from the shadows as Orpheus approached Pluto on his throne.

"Whose music brings my kingdom to a standstill?" asked Pluto, annoyed.

"Mine, a poet's," said Orpheus boldly. "I've come to borrow back what you've stolen—"

Pluto interrupted. "I *steal* nothing! From the day that men and women are born on earth, they're mine to take when I please. And that includes Eurydice. And now that *you're* here, Orpheus—"

Before Pluto could finish, Orpheus picked up his lyre and began to play a song as large and deep and sad as Death itself. Persephone wept silently into her handkerchief. A tear, hard as crystal, fell from Pluto's eye and rolled across the floor like a marble.

Persephone stared at Pluto, astonished.

"That's the first tear he's ever shed!" she cried.

"Please, Orpheus, no more!" begged Pluto. "Ask what you will, make your demand, but no more sad songs, or I fear I shall dissolve."

"Give Eurydice back to me," my husband pleaded.

"Done," said Pluto quickly, "on one condition. You must not look at Eurydice, or speak to her, until you reach earth's upper air. If you do, she'll be spirited back to hell. There will be no second chance for her or you. Go now, and I will have her follow."

"But how will I know—" began Orpheus.

"You must have faith! Now go!" commanded Pluto.

So Orpheus set off. With a nod from Pluto, I stepped out from the shadows and followed without a sound. Up and up and up, we took the same twisting path that Orpheus had followed coming down. This time, Orpheus didn't sing.

Limping, my ankle aching from the viper's sting, I struggled to keep up. Gradually the tunnel began to grow lighter. I saw daylight above us. We were almost there!

Ahead of me, Orpheus stood in the cave's mouth in bright outline. Then, as in a dream, I watched him step impatiently into the light—

"Eurydice, we're back!" he shouted joyfully, wheeling around to take my hand. Too soon! I still stood in darkness.

With a low roar, the entrance to the cave closed tight, and Pluto appeared, a cold smile on his face. He put his hand on my shoulder and firmly steered me back to the underworld.

Now Orpheus wanders the earth more inconsolable than ever. His sad songs and poems have made him famous, but they give him no comfort.

Persephone tries to cheer me up. She says it's only a matter of time before my husband dies and joins me here. Small consolation!

I've begun writing poems. If Orpheus can, I can too. In hell there's little enough else to do. Would you like to hear one?

I cannot touch you now,
or see your face,
and yet I live—
if shadows live—
for your embrace.

A time will come
when time will drop away.
I dream each night
we walk—two shades—
in timeless twilight.

But the dream ends.
Gray turns to black.
Again I wake and ask:
O Orpheus,
why did you look back?

CAST OF CHARACTERS AND PLACES

(*The Roman names for the Greek gods and goddesses are given in parentheses.*)

AEGINA: Daughter of the river god Asopus, she was changed by Zeus into an island off the coast of Greece.

AEOLUS: King of Thessaly and keeper of the winds. He was the father of Halcyone.

AMALTHEA: The goat who nursed Zeus as an infant. Some say she was the mother of Pan.

ANAXARETE: A noble lady who so cruelly rejected her suitor Iphis that he took his life. She was turned into stone by the gods as punishment for her haughtiness.

APHRODITE (Venus): Goddess of love and beauty. She had no parents, but sprang from the foam of the sea. In some stories she is the wife of Hephaestus (Vulcan). The sparrow, swan, and dove were her birds. The myrtle was her tree.

APOLLO: God of light and truth, prophecy, music, archery, and healing. Often pictured with a lyre, he was a master musician who always spoke the truth and revealed the divine will of the gods to mortals. His tree was the laurel, his creatures the dolphin and the crow. He retains the same name in Roman mythology.

ARACHNE: A vain mortal girl who challenged the goddess Athena to a weaving contest and lost. As punishment, Athena changed her into a spider.

ARCADIA: A remote part of ancient Greece known for its peaceful countryside and simple way of life.

ARCAS: The son of Zeus and the maiden Callisto. After many trials, he and his mother found peace in heaven as the constellations Ursa Minor and Ursa Major.

ARES (Mars): God of war, son of Zeus and Hera. He was disliked by the gods because of his violent ways. The vulture, dog, and wolf were his animals.

ARTEMIS (Diana): Goddess of the moon and hunting, and protector of women. The twin sister of Apollo, she chose never to marry. The cypress was sacred to her, and all wild animals, especially the deer.

ASOPUS: A river god and father of Aegina.

ATHENA (Minerva): Goddess of wisdom, victory, and handicrafts. The favorite child of Zeus, she sprang from his head full grown and dressed in armor. She was the protector of cities and civilized life. The olive was her tree, and the owl her bird.

AURORA: Goddess of the dawn, also known as Eos. She asked Zeus to give her husband, the mortal Tithonus, eternal life, but forgot to ask that he also be given eternal youth.

BACCHUS: See Dionysus.

BAUCIS: In Roman mythology, the devoted wife of Philemon. She and her husband, poor cottagers, entertained Jupiter and Mercury so hospitably that they were granted their wish to die together. They were changed into two trees, a linden and an oak, growing from the same trunk.

CALLIOPE: See Muses.

CALLISTO: A maiden in Artemis' hunting party who had a son fathered by Zeus. She was changed into a bear by Zeus' jealous wife, Hera, and later became the constellation Ursa Major.

CERBERUS: Pluto's three-headed watchdog, who guarded the entrance to the underworld.

CEYX: King of Thessaly and husband of Halcyone. He perished in a shipwreck. He and Halcyone were changed into two birds by the gods.

CHARON: The boatman who ferried dead souls across the river Styx to the underworld.

CLYTIE: A nymph who, because of her stubborn love for Apollo, was changed into a sunflower.

DAPHNE: A nymph who was pursued by Apollo and changed into a laurel tree.

DEMETER (Ceres): Goddess of the harvest. A generous benefactor to everyone on earth, she made the fields and orchards yield an abundance of grains, vegetables, and fruits every autumn. When her daughter, Persephone, was stolen by Pluto, Demeter's grief was so great that winter descended upon the earth and nothing could grow.

DIONYSUS (Bacchus): God of wine and revelry, and the other god of the harvest, along with Demeter.

ECHO: A talkative nymph who was condemned by Hera never to speak first, and then to be able only to repeat what others said to her. Her love for Narcissus went unreturned.

ELYSIAN FIELDS: A sunlit part of the underworld made up of beautiful meadows and groves where the souls of heroes, poets, and virtuous men and women lived in peace and happiness.

ENDYMION: A beautiful shepherd, loved by the moon goddess Selene, who fell into an eternal sleep. He retained his youth and beauty, but never awakened.

EPIMETHEUS: One of the twelve Titans, brother of Prometheus and husband of Pandora. He and Prometheus were given the task by Zeus of making men and animals out of earth and clay.

EURYDICE: The short-lived wife of the poet Orpheus.

FATES: The three ancient goddesses of destiny who decided how long a mortal would live. They knew the past and future. *Clotho*, the spinner, spun out the thread of life. *Lachesis*, the disposer of lots, measured the thread and assigned each person a good or evil outcome. *Atropos*, the inflexible one, carried shears and severed life's thread at the moment of death.

HADES: Another name for Pluto; also, the name of the underworld, Pluto's kingdom.

HALCYONE: The wife of Ceyx. After Ceyx's death, she and her husband were changed by the gods into birds (kingfishers). After that, they nested at sea during a calm week in winter called the "halcyon days."

HARPIES: Hideous winged monsters who did Zeus' unpleasant bidding. They hounded humans, stole food, and spoiled what they did not eat. Each had a body that was half woman, half bird, with a hooked beak and claws.

HEPHAESTUS (Vulcan): God of blacksmiths and fire. Peace-loving and kind, he was born lame, the only one of the immortals who was ugly. Armorer and smith for the gods, he fashioned their thrones, chariots, and weapons.

HERA (Juno): Zeus' jealous wife and the queen of Olympus. She was the protector of married women. The cow and the peacock were her sacred animals.

HERCULES: A mighty Greek hero. The son of Zeus and the mortal Alcmena, he was the strongest man on earth. He was renowned for accomplishing twelve seemingly impossible tasks known as the Labors of Hercules.

HERMES (Mercury): The messenger of the gods, god of science and commerce, and master thief. He was the patron to all who lived by their wits: travelers, rogues, and thieves.

He wore winged sandals and a low-crowned winged hat, and guided dead souls to the underworld.

HESPERUS: The evening star, father of King Ceyx of Thessaly.

HESTIA (Vesta): Goddess of the hearth, the symbol of the home. Meals began and ended with an offering to her.

IPHIS: The gentle suitor of Anaxarete. He took his life when she rejected him.

JUNO: See Hera.

JUPITER: See Zeus.

MERCURY: See Hermes.

MEROPE: The wife of Sisyphus, King of Corinth.

MIDAS: A Phrygian king who wished that everything he touched would turn to gold. Bacchus granted his foolish wish, with unhappy consequences.

MORPHEUS: The son of Somnus, the Roman god of sleep, able to change his face and form to look like any person on earth.

MUSES: Nine in number, they were the daughters of Zeus and the Titan Mnemosyne, Memory. They turned their mother's wonderful stories of gods and heroes into poems and songs. *Calliope* was the Muse of heroic poetry and first among the nine; her son was Orpheus. *Clio* was the Muse of history; *Erato*, of love lyrics; *Euterpe*, of music; *Melpomene*, of tragedy; *Polyhymnia*, of hymns; *Terpsichore*, of dance; *Thalia*, of comedy; and *Urania*, of astronomy.

NARCISSUS: A beautiful youth who loved no one but himself. He fell in love with his own reflection in a pool of water.

NYMPHS: Minor nature goddesses who took the form of beautiful maidens. They lived in the forests, meadows, mountains, rivers, and seas.

OCEANUS: One of the twelve Titans, he ruled the oceans of the earth.

OLYMPUS: The mountaintop abode of the Greek gods, surrounded by a wall of clouds kept by the Seasons. Within, as Apollo played his lyre, the gods lived and slept and feasted on nectar and ambrosia.

ORION: A handsome hunter of gigantic stature whom the goddess Artemis (Diana) slew with an arrow. He was placed in the heavens as a constellation.

ORPHEUS: The mortal son of the Muse Calliope and a Thracian prince, he was the most gifted musician and poet on earth. No one, mortal or immortal, could resist the power of his song. He is best known for his unsuccessful attempt to bring his wife, Eurydice, back from the dead.

PAN: God of nature. Part man, part goat, he was a master musician who delighted in playing sweet melodies on his panpipes. Hermes was his father.

PANDORA: Fashioned by the gods to be the perfect woman, she was given beauty, charm, and other talents, and then sent down to earth with a box that Zeus had forbidden her to open. When she disobeyed and opened the box, many evils and sorrows flew out and spread throughout the world.

PERSEPHONE (Proserpine): The radiant goddess of spring and summer, daughter of Demeter (Ceres). She was abducted by Pluto and forced to live part of each year in the underworld.

PHILEMON: In Roman mythology, the husband of Baucis. He and his wife, poor but virtuous, became the keepers of a temple after entertaining Jupiter and Mercury in their simple home.

PITYS: A nymph who, pursued by Pan, was changed into a fir tree.

PLUTO: The god of the underworld who ruled over the dead. Because he was in possession of all the precious metals and jewels buried in the ground, he was also the god of wealth. An unwelcome visitor on earth, he preferred his gloomy palace in the underworld to living on Olympus. Also known as Hades, he retains the same name in Roman mythology.

POMONA: Roman goddess of fruit trees. She married Vertumnus.

POSEIDON (Neptune): God of the sea, able to both calm the waves and cause terrible storms. He carried a three-pronged spear called a trident. He gave the first horse to humankind.

PROMETHEUS: A Titan who stole the sacred fire of Olympus and carried it down to mortals on earth. As punishment for that and other crimes, Zeus had Prometheus chained to a mountaintop where every day an eagle swooped out of the sky and ate his liver. Prometheus was eventually freed from his torment by Hercules.

SATYR (faun): One of a race of immortal goatmen who lived in the woods and fields. Each had the body of a man but the horns, pointed ears, tail, and legs of a goat. They attended Dionysus (Bacchus) during his wild parties in the forest.

SELENE: Another name for Artemis (Diana), goddess of the moon.

SILENUS: A jovial old satyr, fond of wine and storytelling, who was a schoolteacher and companion to Bacchus.

SISYPHUS: King of Corinth, whose task and punishment in the underworld was to roll a heavy stone up a hill; the stone never stayed in place and always rolled back down again.

SOMNUS: Roman god of sleep.

STYX: The river that dead souls had to cross on Charon's ferry in order to reach the underworld. It was the river of unbreakable oath by which the gods swore.

SYRINX: A nymph who, fleeing Pan, was turned into a reed by her sisters. Pan made her into a musical pipe.

TITANS: Twelve early gods of enormous strength and size who preceded the twelve gods and goddesses of Olympus. Some of them were *Cronus (Saturn)*, Zeus' father, whom Zeus overthrew; *Rhea*, Cronus' wife; *Oceanus* and his wife, *Tethys*; *Prometheus* and his brother *Epimetheus*; *Hyperion*, father of the dawn, and of the sun and moon; and *Themis*, Justice.

TITHONUS: A mortal prince married to the goddess Aurora. He was given eternal life but not eternal youth, so that after many years he shrank and took the form of a grasshopper.

VENUS: See Aphrodite.

VERTUMNUS: Roman god of the changing seasons, especially spring, and of gardens and orchards. His name means "he who changes." He married Pomona.

ZEUS (Jupiter): Ruler of Olympus, whose power was supreme, greater than all the other gods and goddesses combined. He was Lord of the Sky and wielded the thunderbolt. The eagle was his sacred bird, and the oak his tree.

GOFISH

questions for the author

ELIZABETH SPIRES

What did you want to be when you grew up?

I had some interesting career plans when I was five or six. The one I remember best is wanting to be a chimpanzee trainer. I'm glad that I gave up on that.

When did you realize you wanted to be a writer?

When I was twelve, I discovered Emily Dickinson's poetry and Flannery O'Connor's short stories. Those two writers were so inspiring that I decided I wanted to be a writer, too.

As a young person, who did you look up to most?

The authors of my favorite books.

What was your first job?

I began babysitting when I was nine. I also had a paper route in the small town where I grew up. (That's when newspapers were delivered by kids on bicycles.) As a teenager, I worked in the refreshment stand of a drive-in movie theater and behind the soda fountain at a drugstore.

Which of your characters is most like you?

Maybe Emmaline in *The Mouse of Amherst*.

When you finish a book who reads it first?

Usually my husband (who is a novelist).

Are you a morning person or a night owl?

Definitely a morning person.

SQUARE FISH

Where do you go for peace and quiet?

Stonington, Maine. But it's a long drive from Maryland to Maine, so sometimes I just retreat to a quiet space in my mind.

What's your favorite song?

"Ain't No Mountain High Enough" sung by Diana Ross.

Who is your favorite fictional character?

I have several. The Japanese artist in Elizabeth Coatsworth's book *The Cat Who Went to Heaven* and Miss Hickory in Carolyn Bailey's book of the same title. And maybe the main character in Elizabeth Bishop's poem "The Man-Moth."

What are you most afraid of?

Getting so far behind I never catch up.

What time of year do you like best?

Fall is definitely my favorite season. (Spring is amazing but too brief.)

If you were stranded on a desert island, who would you want for company?

Can the "who" be a "what"? If so, I'd take *The Collected Later Novels of Willa Cather.*

If you could travel in time, where would you go?

I wrote a book, *I Heard God Talking to Me*, about the African-American stone carver William Edmondson (1874–1951). If I could travel in time, I'd travel to William Edmondson's yard in Nashville, Tennessee, during the 1930s, look at all of his incredible sculptures, buy one, and bring it back with me to the present.

What's the best advice you have ever received about writing?

I think it's probably best if writers trust their own instincts and not depend on advice.

What do you want readers to remember about your books?

That I wrote about the things that really mattered to me.

What would you do if you ever stopped writing?

I'd hike the Appalachian Trail, spend more time kayaking and snorkeling, and spend four or five months in Japan.

What do you consider to be your greatest accomplishment?

My daughter (except she is totally her own person so I can't really describe her as *my* accomplishment).

Where in the world do you feel most at home?

Here in Baltimore, Maryland, where I live. But if I could have a second home, I think I'd choose Venice.

What do you wish you could do better?

I wish writing came easily to me, but it doesn't. I do a lot of rewriting when I'm working on books and poems.

GO FISH

MORDICAI GERSTEIN

What did you want to be when you grew up?
Tall enough to touch the clouds, or a tap dancer.

When did you realize you wanted to be a writer/illustrator?
When I was about forty.

What's your first childhood memory?
Sitting in my high chair with my parents' huge faces smiling at me.

What's your favorite childhood memory?
My neighbor, Jack Nathan, telling me what *the movies* are.

As a young person, who did you look up to most?
My father and my uncle Phil.

What was your worst subject in school?
Math.

What was your best subject in school?
Art.

What was your first job?
Working in a wholesale grocery warehouse with my father.

How did you celebrate publishing your first book?
We had an opening party after a signing at a bookstore in Greenwich Village.

Where do you write your books?
In my studio.

Where do you find inspiration for your writing?
Everywhere (hopefully).

Which of your characters is most like you?
Arnold of the Ducks, and all the others too.

When you finish a book, who reads it first?
Susan, my wife.

Are you a morning person or a night owl?
I love to stay up late, but I can't because I love to write early in the morning.

What's your idea of the best meal ever?
Anything at the Buca da Orafo in Florence, Italy.

Which do you like better: cats or dogs?
Dogs, though only certain ones. I like foxes better than either.

What do you value most in your friends?
Listening, making me laugh, and telling me everything.

Where do you go for peace and quiet?
On my bicycle.

What makes you laugh out loud?
Stuff that's really silly and really stupid, like John Marshal's drawings and Monty Python, for example.

What's your favorite song?
"Stardust."

Who is your favorite fictional character?
Mary Poppins and Plastic Man.

What are you most afraid of?
People.

What time of year do you like best?
September.

What is your favorite TV show?
Nature.

If you were stranded on a desert island, who would you want for company?
Susan.

If you could travel in time, where would you go?
Back to my childhood to meet my parents and myself as a child.

What's the best advice you have ever received about writing?
Write a first draft without looking back, then put it away for a week before reading it.

What do you want readers to remember about your books?
What each finds most memorable.

What would you do if you ever stopped writing/illustrating?
Ride my bike, play the banjo, paint pictures, raise vegetables, and cook.

What is your worst habit?
You don't want to know.

What do you consider to be your greatest accomplishment?
Winning the Caldecott.

Where in the world do you feel most at home?
Everywhere that I've been happy.

What do you wish you could do better?
Make music and speak foreign languages.

What would your readers be most surprised to learn about you?
I don't like having pets, but I love seeing wild animals (in the wild).